CAPTAIN PUGWASH AN
THE BIRTHDAY PAR

John Ryan was born in Edinburgh and spent much of his early life abroad and at boarding school in England. After war service in Burma he taught art at Harrow and became a contributor to *Eagle* magazine, then in its infancy. Captain Pugwash, who later became his most famous creation on television and in picture books, was in fact created for *Eagle*. Other characters include Harris Tweed, Lettice Leefe, Mungo and Midge, Sir Prancelot, and F. the Fathead. John Ryan is married with three children and several grandchildren. He lives in Rye, Sussex, a one-time notorious haunt of smugglers and pirates. He hopes to continue writing and drawing indefinitely . . . if only to avoid being put to work in the garden!

John Ryan

Captain Pugwash and the Birthday Party

PUFFIN BOOKS

PUFFIN BOOKS

Published by the Penguin Group
Penguin Books Ltd, 27 Wrights Lane, London W8 5TZ, England
Penguin Books USA Inc., 375 Hudson Street, New York, New York 10014, USA
Penguin Books Australia Ltd, Ringwood, Victoria, Australia
Penguin Books Canada Ltd, 10 Alcorn Avenue, Toronto, Ontario, Canada M4V 3B2
Penguin Books (NZ) Ltd, 182–190 Wairau Road, Auckland 10, New Zealand

Penguin Books Ltd, Registered Offices: Harmondsworth, Middlesex, England

Published in Puffin Books 1997

10 9 8 7 6 5 4

Filmset in Monotype Baskerville

Made and printed in England by Clays Ltd, St Ives plc

British Library Cataloguing in Publication Data
A CIP catalogue record for this book is available from the British Library

ISBN 0-140-38116-3

Contents

Captain Pugwash and the
Birthday Party

CAPTAIN PUGWASH WAS very excited.
Tomorrow was his birthday, and
already the crew were dressing up the
ship with all the flags they could lay
their hands on.

"Plundering porpoises! Parties, parcels, presents, rum punch! What fun it's going to be," he thought, as he gazed over at the little port in which the *Black Pig* lay at anchor.

Poor Pugwash! Little did he realize that his very worst enemy had taken lodgings in that same town and was also getting ready for the Captain's birthday.

"Ho ho ho!" growled Cut-throat Jake. "'Appy birthday Cap'n, from a friend," he muttered, as he put the finishing touches to the icing on a large and magnificent birthday cake which he had made specially.

"I'll give 'im an 'appy birthday 'e'll remember as long as 'e lives," he went on, planting a single candle in the centre of the cake . . .

". . . which won't *be* very long! Ah-harrh!"

That night, the *Black Pig* lay peacefully
moored in the moonlit harbour. A small
rowing boat slid out from the quayside
with two figures aboard.

One of them tied the boat up under
the stern of the ship, while the other
climbed up to the deck. He had a large
parcel strapped to his back.

He peered through the hatchway over
the Captain's cabin. Down below, he
could see Pugwash fast asleep.

Then he lowered the parcel on the end of a rope, so that it came to rest by the Captain's bedside.

Then the boat, with the two figures in it, departed as silently as it had come . . .

leaving Captain Pugwash happily snoring in his bunk.

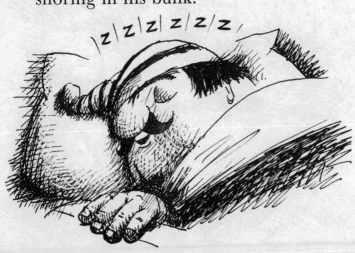

Next morning, Tom the cabin boy arrived in the Captain's cabin with his early morning tea.

"Wakey-wakey, Cap'n," he cried. "Come on! Wake UP!"

"It's your birthday today."

"Whassat?" mumbled the Captain sleepily. "Wh . . . wh . . . why! Capering cuttlefish, of course! It really is MY BIRTHDAY!"

"Congratulations, Cap'n!" said the
Mate who had followed Tom into the
cabin with Pirates Barnabas and Willy.

"*Presents* would be more in order,
Master Mate," replied the Captain
greedily.

"'Ere you are, Cap'n," replied the Mate. "Pair o' bedsocks, wot I knitted meself."

"Bottle o' bubble bath, for your morning tub, Cap'n," said Barnabas.

"And a packet o' jelly babies – except for the ones I've eaten myself," added Willy.

14

"Humph," grumbled Pugwash, "no jewels or gold or silver? How very disappointing.

"But wait! What's this?" he cried, as he noticed the large parcel beside him.

"Now that looks like a real birthday present!"

He unwrapped the parcel eagerly.

"Why, battering barnacles! It's a birthday cake!" he cried. "*From a frend* it says. Well, I have so many friends of course . . .

even if they can't spell 'friend'. I tell you what!

"We'll have a birthday tea party this very evening. Whoopee!" And the Captain danced a merry little hornpipe in his nightshirt to show how happy he was.

Then everybody got ready for the party.

Tom baked
lots of muffins
and scones and
crumpets

and Captain
Pugwash even
squeezed a
penny or two out
of his Black
Piggy Bank . . .

. . . so that the crew could go shopping in the town for fish and chips and sausages and sweeties and balloons and rum.

By evening everything was ready.

The table was laid in the Captain's cabin, groaning with good food and drink.

Gaily coloured balloons hung from the cabin roof, and the birthday cake, with its single candle ready to be lit, was placed at the Captain's end.

Then, as darkness fell, Tom started
serving the food.

The pirates took their places and
started eating and drinking for all they
were worth.

All of them were greedy . . .

but none so greedy as Captain
Pugwash.

Of course nobody even thought of looking out of the ship, so nobody noticed that once again . . .

two figures in a small boat
had rowed out from the
quayside, and were now tying
it up under the Captain's
cabin in the stern of the ship.

Cut-throat Jake just couldn't
bear to stay away from the
birthday party.

He climbed up over the
rudder and peered into the
Captain's cabin window.

"Listen to 'em," he whispered. "Any minute now the old ruffian will light that candle

and then we'd better keep our heads down,

'cos from the moment 'e lights it, the whole bunch of them 'as got just fifteen seconds to live!"

Up above in the cabin,
Captain Pugwash rose to his
feet. He had intended to make
a long speech, all about
himself, but he was too greedy
for that.

He wanted to start
eating his beautiful cake
as quickly as possible, so
all he said was:

"I will now light the candle on this splendid cake, and you shall all sing 'Happy Birthday'."
With that, he took a taper . . .

. . . and lit the candle.

"Happy birthday to you!" sang the
pirates. "Happy birthday to you! Happy
birthday dear Captain –"

But then Tom interrupted. "Quiet, all
of you!" he cried.

For Cut-throat Jake had not been able
to resist joining in, and the cabin boy
had heard him.

So it was Jake's voice, all alone, that
floated up, singing "'Appy birthday to
YOU!"

"I'd know that voice anywhere!" said
Tom, and quick as lightning, he seized
the cake and dashed with it to the
window.

"Stop, stop, Tom!" yelled Captain Pugwash. "My cake! My precious cake!" But Tom didn't stop. He just hurled the cake out of the window as fast as he could.

"GET DOWN EVERYBODY!" he shouted and, as they ducked under the table, they heard . . .

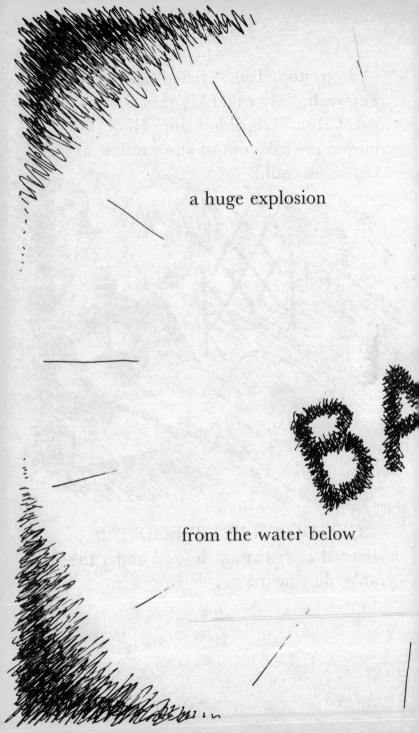

a huge explosion

from the water below

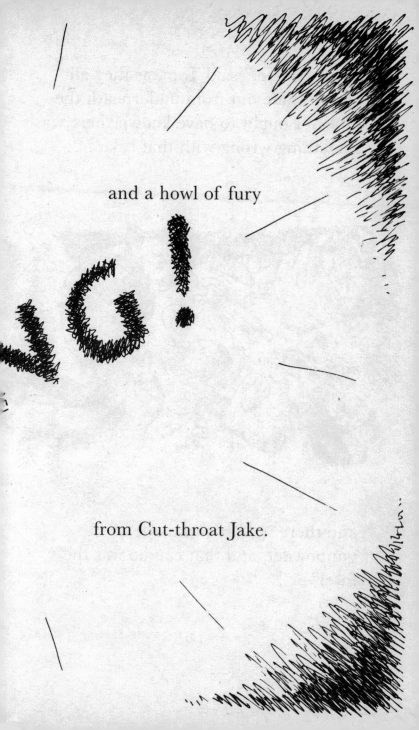

and a howl of fury

ıG!

from Cut-throat Jake.

"Of course," said Tom, as they all
warily came out from underneath the
table. "I ought to have known there was
something wrong with that cake . . .

and there was! It was made of
gunpowder, and that candle was the
fuse!"

Captain Pugwash and his crew and
Tom went over to the cabin window

and looked down through the clouds of
smoke rising from the sea below.

Jake and his mate had escaped
with their lives – but only just
and now they were
      floundering in the water,
      amid the wreckage of
      their boat.

"Tottering turtles! That'll teach them to try their tricks on ME!" boasted the Captain. "But that's all very well. What *am* I going to do for a cake?"

"Don't worry about that, Cap'n," said Tom.

"I never was too happy about that birthday present . . .

so this morning I baked you another cake. Here it is!"

"Tom," said the Captain, "you're coming on! One of these days we'll make quite a useful cabin boy out of you.

"Meanwhile, for the second time this evening, I shall light the candle on my birthday cake."

But even as he did so . . .

. . . there was a loud

shouted all the pirates in great alarm.

But Tom just laughed.
"Don't worry," he said. "This
time . . .

. . . it was only one of the *balloons* – falling on to the candle!"

Captain Pugwash and the
Sunken Silver

ON THE DECK of the *Black Pig*, the
Captain's crew were puzzled.

"What ever can 'e be up to?" asked
the Mate.

"Dunno," answered Pirate Barnabas,
"but wot ever it is, it's bloomin' noisy!"

"Aye, I couldn't sleep a wink this
afternoon," complained Willy.

For two days now, the sound of loud
hammering and sawing had been
coming from the Captain's

cabin, where Pugwash and Tom were
working together.

And when he came out of his cabin for his meals, there was an especially greedy gleam in the Captain's eye.

"'E's after treasure, that's wot!" grunted Barnabas. But even as he spoke, the others looked around in amazement . . .

. . . as the cabin door opened, and out on to the deck came a most astonishing sight.

It was a barrel on legs, with a window in the front and a pipe from the top, carried by Tom.

"Well I never!" muttered the Mate.
"Whatever 'as 'e got there?"

"This," announced Captain Pugwash,
raising the lid and lowering the barrel
to the deck . . .

". . . is my new underwater treasure-hunting diving suit.

"It's the very latest thing in submarine technology, invented by me, of course — with a little assistance from Tom here.

"Deep down on the
seabed, at the foot of that
sharp rock over there," he
went on, pointing to the
other side of the bay in
which the *Black Pig* lay
at anchor . . .

". . . there lies the wreck of an
old Spanish treasure ship. It is
said that there is a chest of silver
bullion on board. Blistering
barnacles! There's probably
enough booty down there to keep
us in rum for the rest of our lives!

"Until now, nobody has ever
been able to get at it. It
lies too deep for any
ordinary diver to reach it,
and all efforts to raise the
ship have failed.

"But my new
invention has, of
course, changed everything. I myself
am the only one brave enough to
undertake such a perilous mission."

"Greedy enough, you mean!"
muttered Barnabas, but Pugwash
pretended not to hear.

"Leave the suit there on the deck,
Tom," he said, "and you, Pirates
Barnabas and Willy, mount a guard on
it till dawn."

That night,
the Captain
dreamed of
the riches
which would
soon be his . . .

and next
morning, when
Tom came to call
him, Pugwash
was up and
ready for his
great adventure.
But . . .

. . . when he came out from his cabin,
Barnabas and Willy were fast asleep,
and there was no sign of the diving
suit.

"Floundering flatfish!" cried the
Captain furiously. "A fat lot of use you
two are, letting my precious new
invention get washed overboard while
you lie there snoring your heads off!

"It's a bit late to wake up now," he
added, as Willy and Barnabas began to
rub the sleep out of their eyes.

58

"There's only one thing for it. I shall have to make another suit. Come on Tom."

Tom looked thoughtful, as he followed the Captain back to his cabin. "How odd," he said to himself, "the suit disappearing like that. The sea was dead calm last night."

Soon the pair of them were hard at
work again.

This time, the
sound of hammering
and sawing was
louder than ever,
although every
now and
again . . .

OUCH!

. . . the Captain
hammered *himself*
in his haste.

By evening, the second underwater
diving suit was ready.

That night, the Captain kept it safely
in his cabin and hardly slept a wink.

Next morning, before the crew were awake, Tom helped the Captain into the suit.

First, they checked that they could hear each other through the breathing tube.

It wasn't easy
getting the
Captain into
the rowing
boat in his suit,
but at last . . .

Tom got him comfortably settled,
with his sword and his rescue
rope and his breathing tube. Tom
took nothing except for a small
packet which he had picked up
from the galley that morning.

Then, as he rowed the little boat towards the tall rock, Pugwash gave out his instructions through the breathing tube.

We shall tie up by the rock, Tom. I shall descend to the seabed, and you will stand by to pull me up when I have got the treasure chest.

At last they reached
the rock. Tom tied the
boat up, while the
Captain rolled over the
side into the water.

BLACK

SPLOSH!!

Soon he was floating gently down to
the bottom of the sea.

Up above, Tom
carefully tied the
top of the
breathing tube
and the rescue
rope to the boat
while, down
on the seabed . . .

BL PIG

Captain
Pugwash
found himself
standing . . .

Now to find the treasure chest.

... on the deck of the sunken ship.

At first, he found it difficult to move about because

walking under water is quite different

to walking on dry land.

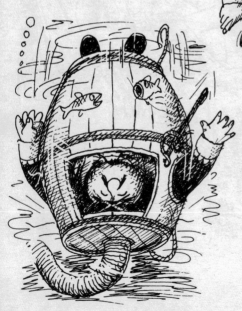

Once he very nearly fainted with fright when a large, fierce-looking fish came to inspect him.

But the fish seemed even more frightened than the Captain was, and swam away as fast as it could.

When Pugwash felt
at ease under the
water, he began his
search.

He looked here.

He looked there.

He looked
everywhere.

And then at last he saw it, hidden
under the bunk in what might have
been the Spanish captain's cabin.

There was a great brass-bound box,
bulging with silver. "I've found it, Tom!
I've found it!" he cried.

Eagerly he began to rummage
through the treasure. "A dinner service
fit for a king," he breathed. He was just
packing it all back in the chest . . .

when he felt a tap on the back of his
diving suit.

At first he took no notice.
"Another of those silly old
fish," he thought.

But the tap came again – louder this
time.
The Captain turned . . . and saw . . .

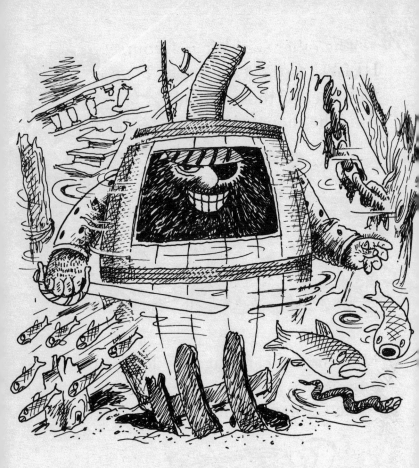

Horror of horrors! His worst enemy,
Cut-throat Jake, also in an underwater
barrel, grinning hideously from ear to
ear and brandishing his cutlass.

"The other suit! Why of course! HELP!" thought Pugwash. Then he realized that there was only one thing for it – he would have to *fight*!

He had a bit of a problem reaching for his sword, but in the end he managed to draw it . . .

. . . and a strange, slow motion
underwater battle began.

Very soon Jake was getting
the better of him . . .

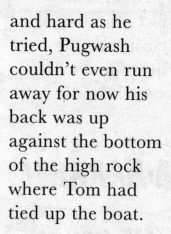

and hard as he tried, Pugwash couldn't even run away for now his back was up against the bottom of the high rock where Tom had tied up the boat.

Up above, Tom could hear the Captain's cries of alarm.

Then, from just round the corner he heard another sound.

Cut-throat Jake's grunts of triumph were coming up through *his* breathing tube which he had tied to *his* boat, on the other side of the rock.

"Ah ha," thought Tom. "I *thought* it might be something like that. Just as well I brought that little packet with me," and he pulled himself towards the other boat . . .

opened the packet, and poured the contents down Jake's pipe.

81

Down on the seabed, Captain
Pugwash thought his last hour had
come. He had dropped his sword, and
Jake had him pinned against the rock.
With a look of fiendish glee, he was
about to cut the Captain's breathing
pipe, when something extraordinary
happened.

Jake fell back,
shut his eyes,
and *sneezed*.

Then he
sneezed again
and again . . .

and again and again and again and
again, for the powder which
Tom had poured
down Jake's
breathing pipe . . .

was PEPPER!

Finally, Jake gave such an enormous sneeze that he blew his diving suit apart, and shot up to the surface.

AA-TTISSHOO!

"Quick Cap'n," called Tom down the pipe. "Tie up the chest and I'll pull you up to the surface!"

So Pugwash did his best to shut the
treasure chest, and somehow tied it to
the side of his diving suit and Tom
pulled him up with the rescue rope.

The little boat was
very low in the water as
Tom rowed back to the
Black Pig, leaving Cut-
throat Jake still sneezing
and swearing in the
water.

ATT·ISS·HOOO

Minutes later, Captain Pugwash
was back aboard his own ship,
surrounded by his admiring crew.
"What did I tell you, eh?" he
boasted. "Rollicking rudders,
there's a king's ransom in that
chest! Why, I might even give you
each a silver spoon!"

"Very generous I'm sure," said the Mate. "But tell us, Cap'n, how did you manage to do it?"

"With skill, courage, endurance – all my usual qualities, Master Mate," replied Pugwash. "And . . . yes, well, I did have a spot of bother with that old fool Cut-throat Jake down there on the seabed, but I soon put paid to his little game. It was easy!"

"SNEEZY more like," thought Tom,
but already he was busy getting the
pirates' breakfast, and he said nothing.